The Chinese Dragon and other Poems about FESTIVALS

Compiled by Andrew Fusek Peters Artwork by Kelly Waldek

First published in 2000 by Hodder Wayland, an imprint of Hodder Children's Books

This paperback edition published in 2008 by Wayland, an imprint of Hachette Children's Books.

Copyright © 2000 Wayland

Wayland
338 Euston Road
London NW1 3BH

Wayland Australia
Level 17/207 Kent Street
Sydney NSW 2000

Editor: Sarah Doughty
Designer: Tessa Barwick
Cover Designer: Fiona Grant

British Library Cataloguing in Publication Data
Peters, Andrew (Andrew Fusek)
The Chinese Dragon and other Poems about Festivals
1. Festivals - juvenile poetry 2. Children's poetry, English
I. Title
821.9'14

ISBN 978 0 7502 5568 4

Printed in China

Acknowledgements: The publishers would like to thank the authors for permission to use their poems in this anthology: poems © the authors.

Wayland is a division of Hachette Children's Books, an Hachette Livre UK company.

www.hachettelivre.co.uk

Contents

It's Festival Time

A festival! A festival!
A friendly, family festival.
The time of year that's best of all.

A festival! A festival!
When food is most digestible,
and games are all contestable,
and presents are requestable.

A festival! A festival!
A friendly, family festival.
The time of year that's best of all.

A festival! A festival!
Sing songs and sound celestial.
Religions east and west have all
got days they call a festival.

A festival! A festival!
A friendly, family festival.
The time of year that's best of all.
A festival! A festival!

Nick Toczek

5

The Chinese

I'm the dragon who dances in the street.
I'm the dragon in the festival.
I leap and twist on caterpillar feet.
I'm the dragon who dances in the street.
I snap and snort and stamp to the beat.
I shiver my scales. I can't keep still.
I'm the dragon who dances in the street.
I'm the dragon in the festival.

Dragon

I'm the dragon of red and green and gold.
I'm King of the Chinese New Year.
I come from the land of stories of old.
I'm the dragon of red and green and gold.
I can breathe out fire or smoke that's cold.
If you've been good, then you've nothing to fear
From the dragon of red and green and gold –
The King of the Chinese New Year.

Catherine Benson

Tossing Pancakes

"Alright!" says dad. "This should be fun.
Now let me show you how it's done.
Just watch what I do, everyone. . ."

Now, why've I got this dreadful feeling
Somehow soon we'll all be peeling
Pancakes off the kitchen ceiling?

Nick Toczek

Easter Egg Hunt

I look for an egg, as round as the earth,
Mary, mother of God, gave birth.

I look for an egg, a tasty surprise,
Jesus, her son, grew up to be wise.

I look for an egg that hides the chick;
Jesus healed the lame and sick.

I look for an egg, but help, it's lost!
Jesus died upon the cross.

I'm happy, I've found eight, nine, ten!
Jesus has come to life again!

Tasty egg with chocolate shell,
Let us give thanks, all shall be well.

Andrew Fusek Peters

The Big Steel Band

There's a carnival
down the street,
and we clap hands
and stamp our feet
to the sunshine sound of the big steel band.

The floats pass by
all through the day,
and costumed people
swing and sway
to the sunshine sound of the big steel band.

There's a dragon
and there's a King!
We wave and laugh
and cheer and sing
to the sunshine sound of the big steel band.

Wes Magee

Hunting The Leaven
Passover

Take a candle, take a feather,
hunt in every crack.
Find each piece of leavened food
and quickly bring it back.

We'll clean our home from top to bottom,
clear out all the yeast.
And then we'll lay the table
for our special Seder feast.

Tony Mitton

Holi
Festival Of Spring

The bonfire roars.
Flames redden my face.
Our coconut's roasting
at the base.
Dad's telling the story
of Prahlad the good
while sparks fly up
from the crackling wood.

I love the bonfire's
fierce heat
and the special sweets
we get to eat.
But even better
than wood-scented smoke
are the stories of Krishna
and how he would joke.

We can do tricks
like the ones Krishna played,
throwing powder and being
splashed and sprayed.
Everyone screams and laughs
as they run.
Getting covered in colours
is always such fun!

Penny Kent

Baisakhi Harvest Festival

Baisakhi, Baisakhi,
three days long, (hold up three fingers)
a party for harvest
with feasting and song. (Wave hands from side to side)

We'll dance to the banghra
with tingling feet, (lift feet one by one in dance)
and all our new people
will sip the amrit. (Sip delicately from imaginary vessel)

With music and hymns
hear our festival ring, (put up hand to ear)
as we honour our Guru,
the great Gobind Singh. (Give appropriate Sikh
gesture of reverence.)

Tony Mitton

Dance of May

Skipping with our ribbons,
gripping on the ends,
skipping with our ribbons,
weaving round our friends.

Bandaging the Maypole,
blue and red and white,
bandaging the Maypole
'til it's criss-cross tight.

'Til we're tied together
on this merry day.
'Til we're tied together
by the dance of May.

Gina Douthwaite

Great Independence Day!

Today was Independence Day,
   the Fourth day of July.
Dad put up the Stars and Stripes
   and mum baked apple pie.
I wore my cowboy boots and hat.
   The sun shone in the sky.

We held a square dance on the lawn.
   Those fiddlers! They could play!
We ate our fill of hot dogs
   as we sat on bales of hay.
That night I flopped in bed and said,
   "Great Independence Day!"

Wes Magee

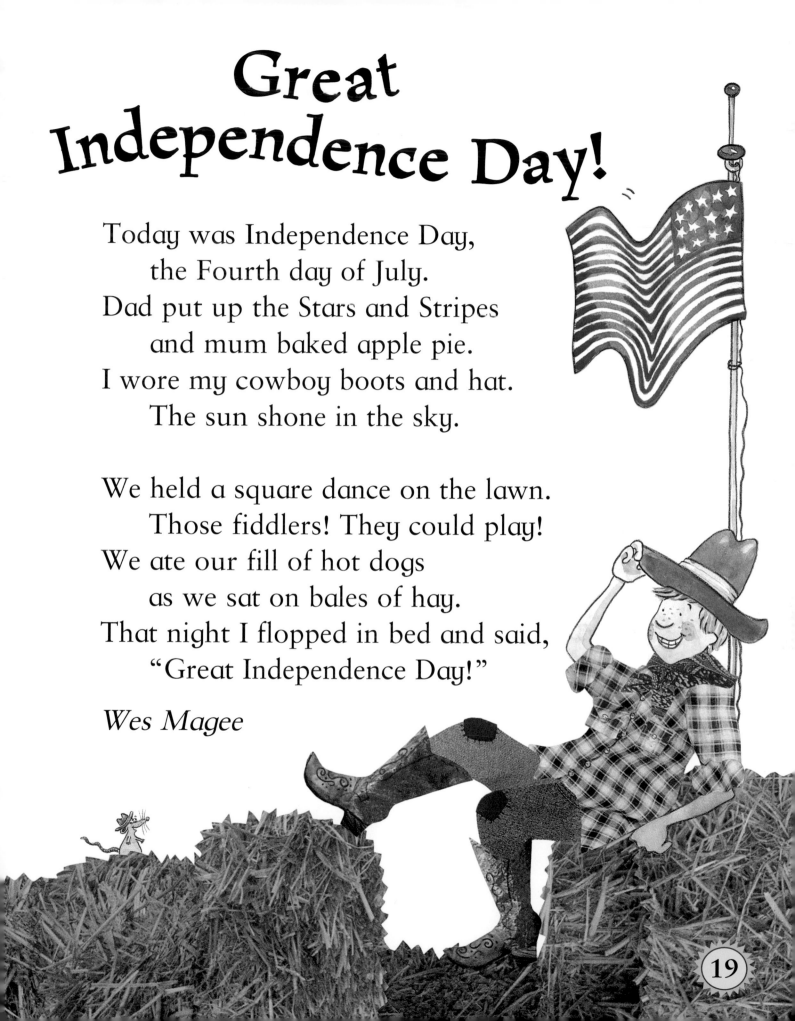

Raksha Bandhan
Brothers And Sisters Day!

Anil, my brother, can be a real bossy-boots.
Sometimes we argue, sometimes we fight.
He wants this, and I want that,
And each of us always thinks we're right!

But at Raksha Bandhan
I will plait him a rakhi
Which I'll tie round his wrist
To keep him from harm.

He'll give me a present
And swear to look after me
(Last year he gave me
A tiny gold charm).

It's our special day to remember each other,
Fall-outs and fights don't matter, you see.
I know I really care about Anil
And Anil cares about me.

Patricia Leighton

20

Hallowe'en

The pumpkin has an orange skin.
When the candle is put in,
its gums show
in the glow
and it gives a silly grin.

Jill Townsend

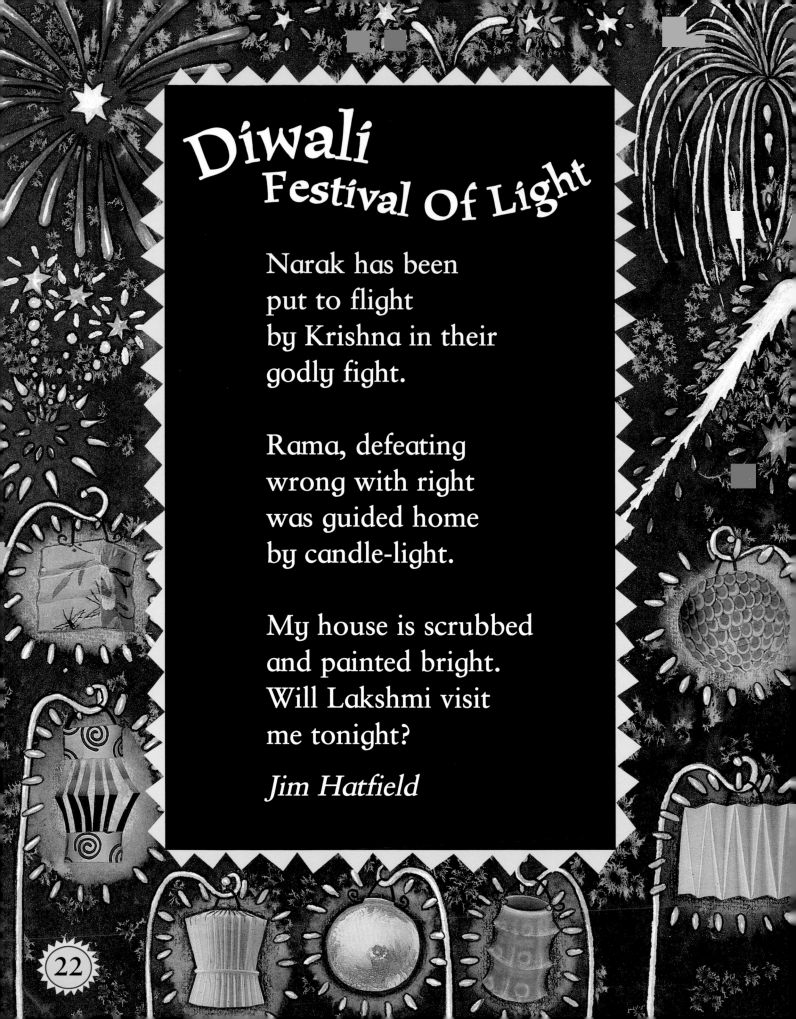

Diwali
Festival Of Light

Narak has been
put to flight
by Krishna in their
godly fight.

Rama, defeating
wrong with right
was guided home
by candle-light.

My house is scrubbed
and painted bright.
Will Lakshmi visit
me tonight?

Jim Hatfield

Offrenda
Day Of The Dead

Make a skull of marzipan,
Bake a bone of bread,
Take a picnic to the graveyard
On the Day of the Dead.

Bring a chocolate coffin,
Bring an almond cake,
Lay them on the tombstone
For when the dead awake.

The friendly dead are smiling
And remembering the sun
The taste of milk, the fire of chillis
How it felt to sing, to run.

And when the night has fallen,
On the gravestones candles burn . . .
We think of how we came from earth
And to the earth return.

Jan Dean

Poor Guy Fawkes

Slumped in a cart,
His head a swede,
"Penny for the guy!"
The children plead.

And on the Fifth,
As flames lick higher,
He twists and writhes,
His clothes catch fire.

"Look, look, the guy!
His hat's aflame!"
The children dance
And chant his name.

From head to toe,
Now burning bright,
As fireworks split
The misty night.

24

Poor Guy Fawkes,
Now just an ember.
He'll burn again
Next November.

Eric Finney

25

Ramadan

A time for thinking,
prayer and praise
with holy scriptures
to end the days.
Fasting, and reading
from the Koran,
during the month
of Ramadan.

Jill Townsend

Id-Ul-Fitr
A Skipping Chant
For The End Of Ramadan

Ramadan
Ramadan
New Moon
New Moon
Break the fast,
Break the fast!

Samora, pakora,
pamosa, samosa,
tappati, chappati,
sambal, poppadom,
NOW!

Judith Nicholls

Christmas Eve

Wes Magee

It's Christmas Eve
in bed you lie,
and one new star
shines in the sky.

. . . and Christmas Morning

Wes Magee

When morning dawns
you'll wake to see
stacked presents round
the Christmas tree.

Why Santa Claus Sometimes Prefers The Front Door

He remembers
Those Decembers
Burning embers,
Chimney holes,

When he splendid-
Ly descended,
But rear-ended. . .
   On the coals!

J. Patrick Lewis

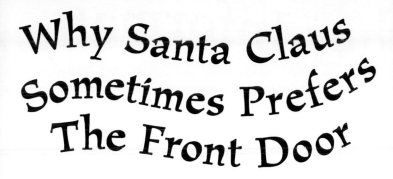

Further Information

After reading a poem (either as a group or individually), ask the children if they know about the festival the poem refers to and if there are any words in the poem they do not understand.

These poems are an opportunity to introduce themed work around a particular festival and there are some good titles that can help for reference material relating to particular festivals (see the books to read list).

Children might want to add movement to the poems. 'Chinese Dragon', 'The Big Steel Band' and 'Id-Ul-Fitr' (the Skipping Rhyme) are particularly good for this, and it may help to learn the poems off by heart in order to do the actions. The author has added the actions to 'Baisakhi' which would work well for performance at assembly.

Food is an important element in many festivals. The children can ask relatives about the types of food and how they are prepared. Do they have any good family tales? (Such as in the poem called 'Tossing Pancakes'). Are there any special rituals that go with food preparation? What foods do children recognise? (see 'Id-Ul-Fitr – Skipping Chant'). The school can do a themed day in co-operation with the catering staff to produce food relevant to a festival.

The *Like-A* game is a way of turning these observations into poetry. If you toss a pancake – can you describe how high it goes? Perhaps "As high as a skyscraper". If samosas are hot – how hot are they? "Hot like a furnace"? Or "Like my brother's face when he's angry"? You can do this with any festival-related nouns.

In 'Holi', the author refers to Prahlad and Krishna. Find out about them and other characters such as Nanak and Lakshmi. Encourage the children to find out the stories behind each festival – what is Independence Day? Why do we dance around the Maypole? Why do we burn Guy Fawkes? Some of the traditional stories can be acted out with costumes.

'Why Santa Claus Sometimes Prefers The Front Door' could lead on to a group poem about all the different ways Santa could get into the house – up the drainpipe, through the plughole; the more impossible, the better!

The above activities will promote and reinforce the suggested work at various levels in the National Literacy Strategy and provide cross-curricular links.

About the Poets

Catherine Benson spent her childhood in Scotland, where she grew up loving the countryside and all nature. She lives in Bradford and often writes about nature. She also paints, enjoys reading and sitting with her cat, Chivers, on her lap.

Jan Dean lives in Knutsford. She likes cooking and is good at puddings. She writes poems and stories, especially spooky stories. For fun, she reads, sings in the church choir, invents mad games for Beaver Scouts and walks the dog.

Gina Douthwaite lives in an old house where blacksmiths used to shoe horses. Cows lean into her garden to chew the hedge. There's a pond with ducks, fish and sometimes a heron! All around are woods and hills where she walks her dogs and watches foxes and pheasants.

Eric Finney lives and used to teach, in Ludlow in Shropshire. He has written hundreds of poems about school. His best ideas for poems come when he walks over the nearby hill-fort or when he sits on his back lawn under the big walnut tree.

Jim Hatfield lives in an untidy house near the Wrekin Hill in Telford and works at a library nearby. He writes poems, books and lots of letters. He likes everything, except wallpapering, but especially loves telling stories to children in schools.

Penny Kent was born in Surrey and at present lives in a little farming village in Bavaria with her husband, son and daughter. She has had poems published in a variety of children's books.

Pat Leighton lives in Bromsgrove, Worcestershire, with a fat cat called Lucy. She likes walking, daydreaming, being nosy and writing poems, of course. When she was nine, she cut the poetry pages out of a whole set of encyclopedias and got into BIG trouble!

J. Patrick Lewis is a retired college professor and now full-time author and elementary school visitor who lives in Chagrin Falls, Ohio (USA) where he is happily disguised as a children's poet. He has thus-far published over 30 children's picture and poetry books.

Wes Magee lives in a cottage on top of the North Yorkshire Moors with two cats (Rusty and Fox) and lots of fish in the wild stream that runs through his hillside garden.

Tony Mitton lives in a small house in Cambridge with his wife, two children and their cat, Twiggy. He used to be a primary school teacher, but now writes poems and stories for children, including his latest collection *he Red & White Spotted Handkerchief* (Scholastic).

Judith Nicholls lives in a very old cottage in a Wiltshire churchyard. She has written about forty books and visited over five hundred schools. Her poems are sometimes mysterious, sometimes funny, about animals, people – and much more. She likes gardening, walking and eating carrot cake!

Andrew Fusek Peters has performed his poetry and stories in thousands of schools. His books include *Sheep Don't Go To School* (Bloodaxe) and *Sadderday and Funday* (Hodder). He loves walking and fiddly gadgets.

Nick Toczek performs the world's fastest poem, makes up cool stories, does mean magic tricks, tells dreadful jokes, and argues with his dangerous puppets.

Jill Townsend lives with her husband and an elderly Scottie dog near a forest in Hampshire, so quite a lot of her poems are about trees. She also likes walking, listening to music and seeing operas.

Books to Read

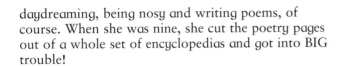

Let's Celebrate: Festival Poems. A collection of Festival Poems edited by John Foster (OUP). A wide variety of festivals with accompanying notes in a lively and colourful anthology.

A Christmas Treasury: Very Merry Stories and Poems by Kevin Hawes (Harper Collins). A selection of stories and poems.

The Usborne Book of World Religions by Susan Meredith (Usbourne). Explains the differences between world religions.

We Love series (Wayland). A series of ten books on religions and festivals, explaining the background to different cultures and the ways they are celebrated.

Seasons Of Splendour; Tales, Myths And Legends Of India by Madhur Jaffrey (Pavilion Books). Stories and background to Holi, Diwali and other festivals.

Festivals, Family and Foods by Diana Carey (Hawthorn Press). Takes you through the festivals of the year with crafts, recipes, activities, songs and stories.

Picture acknowledgements: Bill Pugliano/Getty 13; Peter Sanders 26; Tony Stone Worldwide 11, Wayland Picture Library 17.

Index of First Lines